DARK & STRONG

HAUNTED TALES FROM THE COFFEE HOUSE

ISBN: 978-0-9839069-9-5

Cover Concept, Artwork and Design: J.H. Glaze
Photography: Susan Grimm & J.H. Glaze
Text Editing: Susan Grimm

First Printing March 2015
Published by MostCool Media Inc.
"Make it interesting. Make it MostCool."

Proudly printed in the United States of America.

First Edition March 2015

10 9 8 7 6 5 4 3 2 1

If you enjoy this story, you may want to try the full-length novels, novellas and short stories by J.H. Glaze. Available on Amazon.com & other online retailers in eBook and Paperback.

Adult Horror:

Novels:

The Spirit Box: John Hazard Book I

NorthWest: John Hazard Book II

Send No Angel: John Hazard Book III

Ghost Wars: John Hazard Book IV (*Coming Soon*)

Short Stories:

The Horror Challenge Volumes I-III

Compendium: The Horror Challenge Collection

Special Novellas:

Night of the Living Inflatable Love Dolls

Forced Intelligence: A Novella.

The Life We Dream: A Novella.

Serial Novel: YA & Adult

RUNE: The Thriller Series

RUNE: The Complete First Season

Visit the pages of JH Glaze:

www.JHGlaze.com

Facebook: Author JH Glaze

Follow on Twitter: @themostcoolone

Search for JH Glaze on Google for more!

Thanks For Reading! Reviews on Amazon and other sites are greatly appreciated. Please tell your friends about Author J.H. Glaze books.

DARK & STRONG

HAUNTED TALES FROM THE COFFEE HOUSE

J.H. GLAZE

Just a Wisp of a Woman

Written at Land of a Thousand Hills Coffee
Roswell, GA.

"What can I get you?" the barista asked from behind the counter.

I stood there mute with no excuse for my silence, staring at the handwritten menu posted behind him on a chalkboard on the wall.

"I don't know."

"What do you usually order?" His smile revealed he had encountered customers like me before and learned a trick or two about how to earn a tip where one may have not been forthcoming. If nothing else, he could expedite my order to serve those forming a line behind me.

"Uh... I usually get the frozen blended drinks." I tried not to hesitate too long on the response, but I did not recognize the names of the beverage offerings.

The drinks I would have considered were named after countries rather than the traditional big chain name of something – something fancy. Here, I had a choice between a Rwanda and a Samoa.

"What's the difference? Is the Samoa larger?" I attempted a joke playing on the way that Samoans are often known to be large people, but it fell on deaf ears and resulted in a blank stare before he continued with a description of the drinks.

"French press." My companion knew what she wanted and she told him while I waffled.

"Huh?" Susan had selected this location, and likely looked at the menu online to make her choice before we even arrived. It was unusual for her to make up her mind so quickly.

"The Rwanda is chocolate and caramel, while the Samoa is chocolate, caramel, and coconut." He recited the ingredients hoping to relieve my indecision.

Just then, his co-worker stepped out from the shadows and added, "Like the Girl Scout cookies."

"Ahh…" I could visualize that. When I was younger and not as weight conscious, I would have eaten a half box of those delicious treats in one sitting. "Yeah, I'll have the Samoa."

"It's really good." He smiled and turned to my companion. "What size French press would you like, then?"

"Small, please." Susan was sure of herself. I was wondering how small a small would be.

He tapped the order on the screen of the tablet computer and turned it for me to finger my signature. "We'll bring that right out to you."

After adding a tip, I signed illegibly and tapped the button to seal the deal, opting out of the printed receipt.

We turned and walked to the side door to survey the seating options outdoors, but the heat and humidity on this last day of August seemed oppressive for an outdoor session of writing. I suggested we go back inside. "Whatever you want," she agreed.

Back inside, we had the opportunity to check out what we may have missed by ordering as soon as we arrived. The shop was built inside the shell of a very old house. Except for the obvious addition of the work area, the rest of the house had been restored to its original charm. Worn wooden floors lay beneath walls of soft greens and reds dressed in a simple décor that spoke to an African vibe. I don't mean masks and wooden carvings, but a few items including a flag, a map and a squat wooden bicycle-like device that was signed, "A coffee bag transport from Rwanda."

There were plenty of open tables, though some were populated with folks tapping away on their laptop keyboards, deeply involved in whatever it was they were doing. The place was unexpectedly busy. I had not expected as much judging from the unimpressive exterior of the house, which was situated on the street corner atop a small hill.

Glancing around at all of the colorful pictures and posters, I settled in next to a window and pulled our computers from my bag. We set up while we waited for our beverages to arrive, and just as I pushed the power button on my notebook, one of the counter guys showed up with our drinks.

"Your first time here?" he smiled. Undoubtedly, it had been obvious when I was ordering and then as we shuffled around in search of the perfect seat.

"Yes." Not much of a response, but I was ready to taste my Samoa.

I leaned over the cup, breathing in the delicious aroma. On the first sip, the straw clogged. Was it the coconut? I blew into the plastic tube. The next sip was exactly what I had hoped. Indeed, it was more than reminiscent of the decadent caramel and coconut cookie.

Meanwhile, my companion had poured herself a cup from the small glass pot he had brought her. "Mmm," she breathed in the aroma before sipping. "This is good."

How could I not ask for a taste after that? Yes, it *was* good. She had ordered the medium roast and thought that I might like the dark better. However, the medium was good to me, smooth and rich.

Getting back to the business at hand, my computer was ready to go, and I began to write. As usual, time began to blur. Some time later, I was pulled from the story by her voice.

"Look out the window. Over there." Susan pointed to something beyond the clouded glass.

As I turned my head, I noticed a couple sitting at a table near ours. In front of them were several stacks of green paper. Raffle tickets? They were definitely tickets of some sort. I made a mental note to find out what they were doing as soon as I had finished looking out the window as requested.

Immediately, I forgot about everything else

going on around me.

"Is that blood on her legs?"

"Looks like she has scraped her knees," she voiced her concern. "Poor thing."

"Maybe I should go out and ask if she needs help."

I rose from my chair and headed for the door hearing a faint voice from behind me as I stepped outside, "Be careful."

My eyes adjusted to the bright sunshine, and I caught sight of the woman headed up the hill away from the coffee shop. A few steps later, she leaned against a fence to catch her breath, allowing me time to catch up.

"Excuse me, do you need help?" I called out to her.

She turned her head, her black eyes staring in my direction. Blood *was* trickling down her legs, and she appeared very weak. Maybe she had fallen. After all, she had been staggering as though drunk or under the influence of some other substance.

"Yes, maybe you can help me. I locked my keys in my truck... again." She seemed embarrassed as she stepped away from the fence. Just then, I noticed the plastic band around her wrist. It was an ID bracelet, the kind you are given when you are admitted into a hospital.

"Where is your truck?" I asked, trying not to pass judgment on the frail broken human being standing before me. Without a word, she began to walk back down the hill to a driveway of some sort and waved over her shoulder for me to follow.

I hesitated. What if it was a trap? Was there someone else waiting down there to hit me over the head, and then steal my wallet and my phone before leaving me there in the dirt and gravel? However, I had the sense that she truly required help, so I followed her down to the outside of an abandoned building where three rusty trucks and an old car were parked in a row, nearly hidden in the overgrown weeds.

"Which one is yours?" I glanced over at the trucks, but none looked as if they had been driven recently. They all appeared broken down.

"This one."

She walked over to the cab of the one sitting closest to the run down car. It had one of those fiberglass camper tops on the back. She pulled on the door handle to no avail.

"I just got out and closed the door, and then I

remembered, shit, my keys." Her smile revealed crooked yellowed teeth. "Do you have a coat hanger or something? I know a guy that has a metal thing he uses to open doors."

"A slim jim?" I asked as I moved to the driver side of the truck. *I'll bet you do,* I thought, glancing around to see if there was anyone lurking nearby.

"A what?"

"It's a metal tool used to open a locked car door. Cops keep them in their cars sometimes." I looked through the window of the driver side door and coughed as a horrible smell came wafting from the truck. There were clothes, pillows, and empty food containers in the front seat. The inside of the cab looked as if it had been lived in. "Have you been living in this thing?"

"Yeah, for a while. Look, you'd be my hero if you could just get that door open" She smiled as if she meant it. "Do you have a coat hanger?"

I held back a sarcastic comment on her offer. I did not mind helping a stranger, but she looked like she had lived a lifetime of hard knocks. The last thing I wanted to be was *her hero*. Who knew what meaning that could hold for her?

Standing close to the door, I realized that it was open just a crack, as though it had not been shut with enough force.

"Let me look around. Maybe there is something in the back of one of these other trucks I can use."

I stepped carefully between the weeds and poison ivy to peer into the bed of the next pickup. The large double-lidded steel toolbox looked promising, but I was disappointed to find nothing inside when I lifted the first lid. Stepping back, I walked to the other side and opened it to reveal a rusty four-way tire iron. It might be useful for breaking the window, but I did not think it was good for much else.

I turned to check the back of the next truck. There was nothing but rusted engine parts scattered about the floor of the bed. Making my way back to where she was standing, I took another look into the dark crack of the door to her *home*. This time the smell triggered a strong gag reflex.

"Can't you see if you can find a coat hanger?" Her voice broke as though she was about to cry.

"I don't know… where I can find one around here. I might be able to get a cop to open it for you. They carry a slim jim to help people who get locked out, but you probably don't want me to do that."

"No, they don't take kindly to homeless people around here." She looked down sadly.

"Well, I don't know what to do except break the glass. I don't have any tools. I guess you'll have to try someone else who comes by. I'm sorry" I turned to walk away.

"No, wait, mister…" Strangely, her voice faded away in the breeze.

I turned back to look but she was gone. Walking back and forth in front the vehicles, I bent down to search beneath each one. There was no sign of her anywhere. I stood there wondering how she could have gotten away so quickly when it had seemed she could barely walk at all. "What the hell?"

I felt the need to check once more before I left. As I approached the woman's truck, I was overwhelmed again by the strange smell. I walked up to the door and looked in at the front seat. Nothing had changed there, but I had not looked in the back beneath the fiberglass top. The dirty windows concealed whatever was inside and I thought it impolite to look closer while she was standing right there beside me. Now I used my hand to wipe the dirt away and leaned to peer inside.

Curled up in a fetal position was the woman who only moments before had been standing there offering to make me her hero if only I could open her locked door. There was no mistaking that it was the same woman. She was wearing the same clothes, and I could see the plastic bracelet on her shriveled wrist. She looked badly decomposed. Considering the condition of the body, I was certain she had been dead for some time.

I turned away from the truck and reached into my pocket for my phone. I wasn't sure if anyone would believe my situation, but I pressed the button to wake it and dialed 911.

"911, what's your emergency?" the man on the line asked.

"I need to report a dead body. There's an old woman in the back of a truck."

"What's your location, sir?"

"I… don't know. Wait a minute, I need to walk to the corner to find the street sign."

"Can you tell me what happened, sir?"

"What?"

"Are you certain she's dead?"

I tried to think of what to say. A lump was forming in my throat and my hands began to shake. It was beginning to dawn on me that I had just experienced something beyond the normal realm of this world.

"Sir, do you know how she died?"

I stopped in my tracks. How was I going to answer the question?

"Sir?"

The answer finally came to me just before I gave him the name of the street.

"She didn't say, but I believe she probably died simply because no one cared." I gave him the address, "Nine sixty-nine, Lone Way." and disconnected the call. I knew Susan was waiting for me, and I hurried back to tell her the tale.

The Inspiration for Just a Wisp of a Woman:

We had lunch in Roswell, GA that afternoon at The Spiced Right Rib House, a great barbecue restaurant. As we were leaving, our GPS indicated we should turn right instead of left. We were looking for Land of a Thousand Hills Coffee Shop and almost as soon as we made the turn, the GPS told us we were going the wrong way. A few blocks up, I made the first left. As we began down the hill, there was a woman walking toward us.

I can say that the description of her in the story was accurate. She was injured and living in a pickup truck in which she had locked the keys. I did try to help her open it, but to no avail. When I left the woman, she was alive and well, though rather drunk. Walking back to the car, the idea came for using this experience as the basis for the first story of the Dark and Strong tour. Susan agreed and so it was.

Phantasmagorical Bakery

Written at Sugar Hill Bakery and Café
Sugar Hill, GA

"You missed the turn. We were supposed to take that road back there." Rose checked the GPS screen, which was flashing, *"Recalculating Route."*

"What the hell! You're supposed to be watching that thing. I can't drive and watch at the same time on these mountain roads." Will scanned the narrow road ahead for a place wide enough to turn around. "You want me to run off one of these cliffs?"

Only if you stop and let me out first. She kept her thoughts to herself as she gazed out the window at the bushes flashing by. There wasn't much else to see except the occasional rocky outcropping on this narrow road. From the drivers seat a view of the valley below would have been beautiful, but from her perspective there was nothing to see.

There was barely enough room on the road for two cars to pass. Every head to head encounter had resulted in a slow careful crawl with a close eye on the mirror lest it be torn off in a moment of carelessness.

"I think there's a place up ahead where we can turn around."

Slowing as he came upon a widening in the road, he rolled to a stop.

"You'll have to get out and watch for me so I don't run a tire off the road."

He sat glaring at her waiting for her to open the door.

"What?" She had been daydreaming about the car traveling at a high rate of speed, missing a curve and launching through the void as it jumped a cliff with her loving husband gripping the wheel, screaming like a little girl. Her own death would be little sacrifice to escape the prison of her depressing life, and at least she could enjoy those final seconds.

"I said, get the hell out and watch so I don't run off the road."

He tried to reach to the other side of the car and grab the door handle but his fat belly got hung up on the console that divided the seats.

"I've got it." Opening the door she climbed out and slammed the door, yelling, "Go ahead."

He put the car in gear and rolled the front wheel off the road headed uphill before turning the wheel sharply in the other direction. Slowly he drove in a tight circle until the car was headed back down they way they had just come. He had an overwhelming urge to keep going and leave her standing there. Instead, he sighed and stopped to wait for her to climb back in.

"Now pay attention for a change. I have to go back to the last side road and turn, right?"

"Yes, but you'll be turning left."

"Of course, I'll be turning left. What else would I do?"

You could get out and jump, she thought, but she said nothing.

For the next several miles, there was cold silence between them. Finally, he asked, "Did we come this far before? It doesn't seem like it should be taking so long to reach the turn."

"The GPS hasn't indicated anything about turning." She tapped it to make sure it wasn't asleep or broken.

Almost on cue, the GPS replied, "Turn left in … fifty feet."

He made the turn and drove into the thick forest that darkened the road ahead. A blanket of fog dipped into the trees, making it even more difficult to see.

"Where the hell did this fog come from? There was nothing but sun when we were traveling the side of the mountain." He leaned forward on the seat, hanging his hands over the steering wheel, straining to see the road in front of them. It was impossible. He reached for the switch to light the headlamps of the car.

"Maybe we should look for a place to stop for a few minutes. I really need to use the bathroom." She shifted uncomfortably in her seat.

"Why didn't you go before we left the motel? I clearly remember telling you to go."

"Of course I did, Will. My bladder isn't what it used to be. Since we turned fifty, things just don't work as well as they did when we were younger. You know what the doctor said." She turned to stare out the window again, squinting at what she thought was a sign ahead.

As they approached, she could read it. *Anna's Magical Bakery and Emporium, 500 Ft.* The letters were painted in fancy script and it was a very attractive sign for a place in the middle of nowhere.

"Did you see that sign? There's a bakery ahead." She put her hand on his thigh. "Let's stop. We can get some coffee and a cupcake or something."

"I didn't see any sign. Why would there be a bakery up here in the middle of nowhere?" With a glance, he could see her checking the GPS.

"It isn't on here." She looked up and pointed as she added, "but... there it is!"

The worn wood siding gave the small building the appearance of age, but it was well maintained. Situated on a large gravel parking lot, it sat in front of an old Victorian house complete with a large front porch and wooden shutters. Reluctantly, Will turned into the entrance.

"I don't want to be here long. We still have at least three hundred miles to go today."

"I'll just use the ladies' room, and then we can get a coffee to go. Okay?"

"Yeah, sure."

He put the car in park and turned off the ignition. She climbed out and waited for him before walking to the entrance door. It opened easily as she took the handle, and a gust of warm air rushed out at them, bringing with it the smell of fresh pastry and flowers.

Once inside, she was astounded at the place. It was much larger on the inside than it had appeared and was well lit by a combination of old electric lights and a multitude of flickering candles. Along the walls stood antique cabinets made of rich dark wood, every shelf covered with small decorative knickknacks, and draped with garlands of dried flowers and strings of colored glass beads.

Placed strategically around the room were several polished wooden tables of various sizes, sitting atop ornate pedestals and surrounded by luxurious vintage parlor chairs. Along the back wall, an old-style glass display case was filled with fabulous pastries, cakes and cookies, all of them decorated with an artistic flair.

"I've never seen anything like this before, so beautiful," she spoke in a quiet breathy voice. Glancing at her husband of twenty-seven years, she saw his face held a look of disgust.

"This place is a dump." He peered at the old wooden shelves and the collection of cast iron farm animals arranged in no particular order. Looking around, his eyes wandered over the handful of warped tables and rickety chairs. The glass display case of baked goods was cracked, and he squinted at one of the crooked cakes and thought he spotted some mold.

There was a movement just out of his line of sight as three young women approached from the back of the room. Two were brunettes and the third was blond, but they shared one trait. All three had a natural beauty. Will was stunned by their appearance, and he was certain the room was brighter and a little less run down as it had been only seconds before they appeared.

"Welcome to Anna's." The blonde took Will by the arm and walked him to one of the tables. "Have a seat and relax now that you're here. What can I get you to drink?" With a smile, she looked into his eyes and he melted inside. He did not even notice that his wife had been seated directly across from him.

"I wouldn't have expected such a charming place out here in the middle of nowhere." Rose ran her fingers across the top of the rich wooden table.

"It's hard to tell these days, but this used to be quite a busy shop before they put in the highway. Most of the traffic has stopped coming by, but Anna has kept the place running all of these years. Like the name says, it really is a magical place." The young woman pulled her hair back to rest behind her ear. "Would you like some coffee or tea?"

"Oh yes, I would love some hot tea. Do you have jasmine?" Rose did not speak directly to the young girl. Instead, her eyes wandered over the richly embroidered arms of her chair.

"Sure we do..." Again the girl smiled, "and coffee for your handsome friend here?"

That caught Will's attention. Did she just call him handsome? He straightened in his chair and tried to suck in his gut, "Sure, with sugar please."

"Oh, the sweetest sugar for you, kind sir," she purred as she turned to go.

As she walked away, Rose called after her, "Wait. Is there a bathroom I could use?"

"Of course, Rose, follow me." She turned and walked to a hallway as the older woman followed.

"How did you know my name?" she asked the young woman.

"We knew you were coming. Anna was expecting you. We hope you will enjoy it here with us. This is the powder room." She gestured toward the door.

Rose stopped, "I am enjoying it so far. I love

the atmosphere here. You all seem so happy. I have dreamt of a place like this before… so beautiful."

"You never know what can be yours if only you desire it enough." She opened the door and Rose stepped into the luxurious bathroom.

It was decorated as beautifully as the dining area and smelled of spicy perfumes. Next to the old porcelain toilet, a small table held a vintage lamp with a stained glass shade and a book, *Jane Eyre*. Rose picked it up, smiling. It was an old favorite of hers. She pulled down her elasticized slacks and sat atop the warm toilet seat. Opening the novel to the middle, she began to read.

"Just for a minute," she told herself out loud.

Back at the table, Will had been handed a steaming mug of coffee and was taking a sip. For the first time all day, he felt happy. It was the best coffee he had ever tasted and it wasn't too hot to drink. So rich and sweet, he breathed in the aroma as he drank it down. Wiping a drip from his chin, he set the cup on the table.

"That truly was the best coffee I have ever had. May I have a refill?" He looked up to thank the young lady who had served him and saw there were now five girls standing in front of him. Each one could be considered among the most beautiful he had ever seen.

They took each other by the hand and circled around him. He reeled as he felt waves of desire washing over him. What was this magical feeling? He had never experienced anything like it before. He was warm and alive inside for the first time in a long time.

In unison, the women began chanting words he couldn't understand. Yet, they sounded so familiar. Maybe something from a movie... witches... a spell? Suddenly he felt a sharp pain in his gut and a feeling of panic replaced his pleasure.

"No, stop!" he yelled. He tried to rise from his seat and run for the door, but he couldn't do more than stand halfway before his escape attempt was halted by some unseen force.

Meanwhile in the ladies' room, Rose had no idea how long she had been reading, she was enjoying the book so much. She realized that her feet had gone numb and it was probably time she got back to the table. With that, a chill ran up her spine and she shivered.

She wiped away the wetness between her legs with the soft tissue provided on the brass fixture. As she stood to pull up her slacks, she was shocked at how loose they had become. She gasped as she noticed her hands. They were no longer wrinkled and spotted, but had become as smooth and soft as they had been in her youth.

On the wall to the right, there was a mirror and she hurried to look at herself. She squealed at her reflection. The woman looking back at her could be no more than twenty years old. Turning her head from side to side to be sure, she brought her hand up to her face and ran her fingers over her firm chin and up to touch her cheek. Instead of the sagging flesh that she had dreaded for so many years, her skin was smooth and taut. Her hair was long and draped over her shoulders. It shimmered in the soft light with the natural auburn color that she had been unable to duplicate since the first gray hair had appeared many years ago.

Rose gathered the loose fabric of her slacks in her hand and nearly ran out of the bathroom and down the hall to the dining area where she had left her husband. She couldn't wait to see his reaction at the change in her appearance, and she called out, "Will? Honey, you won't believe..."

As she came upon the circle of young women standing around the table, she stopped in her tracks. Will was no longer sitting there. His coffee cup sat empty and he was gone. As she came closer, she saw something on the chair where he had been sitting. It was a cast iron pig, just seven inches tall. The pig stood halfway up on its hind legs and appeared to be dancing.

When the women saw her, they broke the circle and stepped back from the table. They turned toward a gray-haired woman with a youthful face who had stepped into the room from behind the display case. When she moved, it was as though she were floating.

"Welcome to my bakery and our home, Rose. I gathered that you were longing for a change in your life, to be somewhere surrounded by love and appreciation for the true flower you have become. We would welcome you to stay."

Rose was overwhelmed and stood speechless, staring at the pig where her husband had been sitting.

"If you would like to join us here, you may stay as long as you wish. You simply need to pick up your husband here, now in his true form, and place him among the collection of other animals on the shelf."

"You mean… that pig is my… Will?"

"Yes, dear. A fitting choice for him, would you not agree?" The woman smiled.

Rose looked at the pig and back at the woman. She looked again at the pig and then to the group of young women. Without further hesitation, she walked to the chair, lifted the figure of the pig and carried it to the shelf. Setting it among the statuettes of the other farm animals, she announced to the metal gathering before her, "Gentlemen, I would like to introduce you to my former husband, Will."

With that, she patted the pig on the head, then turned and skipped into the waiting arms of the group of giggling young women.

The Inspiration for Phantasmagorical Bakery:

As we drove to the Sugar Hill Bakery, I wasn't sure what I might be writing that day. In an attempt to be inspired, I went looking for a garage sale. I thought I might write about something antique, but we found nothing interesting there.

Rather than waste time looking for another sale, we went directly to the bakery. From the outside, it looked like a run down building that had been painted with bright colors. There was a patio garden, well maintained with flowers and small shrubs, but nothing prepared us for what we would find inside the bakery.

Once we stepped through the doors, we entered a dream world, decorated with all sorts of curiosities and knick-knacks. As you might guess, there were three pretty young women working there, all about the age of twenty with long hair and smiling faces. In the back in the bakery, an older woman with gray hair was working diligently.

The coffee was good and the pastries we enjoyed were fabulous. It truly was a magical place. Now you know how the story idea came to me.

Hamburger
Written at Dancing Goats Coffee Bar
Decatur, GA

Dan woke quickly, as though he'd been shocked by someone dumping a bucket of cold ice water over him. The light in the room was bright and he immediately realized he was lying on the floor. It took a moment for his eyes to adjust as he sat up, and then he saw he was not alone. There were twenty-five to thirty others in this perfect cube of a room with him, all still asleep.

He had no way of knowing where he was, and certainly no idea of how he had come to be here. Sitting there on the floor, he tried to remember something, anything that could explain what had happened, but there was nothing he could pull from memory. He had no recollection at all.

He placed his hands on the floor to keep

himself balanced. It was warm to the touch and he could feel vibration, a kind of humming coming from somewhere below. It was no ordinary sensation, and he felt the short hairs stand up on the back of his neck. He reached back to soothe himself and pulled back a hand wet with sweat.

Just then, there was movement among the many bodies on the floor and an elderly woman pushed herself up to a sitting position and looked around. When her eyes landed on him, she spoke. "Where am I? Can you see my glasses anywhere? I really can't do very well without them." She felt around the floor with her hands with no success.

"Wait there," Dan replied, standing up to step carefully over the others sleeping soundly around him. "I think I see them."

He made his way toward her and picked up the pair of wire-framed glasses lying next to a man curled up on his side. "Here you go."

She took them from him and placed them on her face. "Thank you so much, young man." Looking around, she asked, "Where are we exactly? I am supposed to be home by five o'clock. I'm meeting my new grandson for the first time tonight, and I don't want to be late."

She tried to stand but, after several attempts,

settled back down to the floor. "Who are all of these people? What are we doing here? I don't remember coming into a place like this."

"I don't have any answers, lady. I don't know how I got here either. Can you remember anything?"

"No. I know I was going to the store to get the baby a present, but this is definitely not a place I have ever been shopping before."

"Try to remember. Any idea how we got here?" Dan was checking others on the floor for any clues to explain where they were.

"No, not at..."

Suddenly someone nearby began screaming, "Help me! I think my arm is broken."

A teenaged boy sprang to his feet, his twisted arm hanging limply at his side. He tried to use his other arm to lift it, but it was obvious from the pointed bone poking sharply against the skin near his elbow that the arm was shattered. "Aghhh!"

The boy let go of the useless appendage and grabbed his forehead. "I feel dizzy." He moaned and slumped back to the floor unconscious from the intense pain.

"Hey! Anybody? Somebody help us!" Dan yelled as loud as he could. The sound of his voice was absorbed into the walls as if he had screamed into a pillow.

"I don't think anyone can hear you." The woman looked at him, her eyes wet with tears.

"If no one is out there, then how did we get here and why are we here?" He stepped over the people who lay between him and the nearest wall and began pounding on it with both fists. "Let us out," he yelled.

"What did you say?" The woman called out to him. "Did you say something?"

He stopped pounding and turned to her. "Were you talking to me?" He took a few steps back toward her through the twisted arms and legs of the unconscious.

"I asked if you were saying something, but you didn't answer." She looked perplexed. "Couldn't you hear me?

Now he was confused. He shook his head, "No, I guess I couldn't hear anything while I was shouting. Come to think of it, not even the sound of my fists pounding the wall. It's as though I had stepped into a vacuum."

Dan stepped back to the old woman, pushing the body of another woman to the side so he could sit down next down to her.

"This is such a strange room, mister...."

"Dan, my name is Dan."

"I'm Ruth. It's very nice to meet you, Dan. Especially when no one else here is awake, or maybe alive, except that boy with the broken arm."

"Once you get up close, you can see some of them breathing, but don't worry about that just now. I need you to help me remember what we were doing before we ended up here. Were we together?"

"I don't remember being with you. Let me think back for a minute." She closed here eyes. "I remember getting into my car and driving into town. I think the traffic was light for a weekday. I remember wondering where all the cars had gone. Today wasn't a holiday, was it?"

"No, Labor Day was two weeks ago. At least I think it was. We have no way of knowing how long we've been here."

She sat quietly, then, "I recall finding a parking spot in front of the coffee shop. There were a lot of cars in the lot, but very few people walking about."

"Wait, I remember thinking the same thing. Lots of cars and only a few people walking around."

"Right, and it was very quiet, and then... oh

my."

"What is it, Ruth?"

"I... I'm not sure if I am remembering this correctly, but there was screeching, like a car accident, and a car came flying around the corner... Oh my! Yes, it slammed into the front of the bank building and caught fire."

Dan just looked at her. She was visibly disturbed by her memories. Her lip quivered as more tears began to stream down her cheeks. He felt sorry for her and tried to calm her by rubbing her shoulder. "Maybe it didn't really happen. That sounds like something out of a movie."

"No, Dan, it happened. I'm sure of it. A woman climbed out of the car. Her hair was on fire. She was screaming. She was clutching her... her baby!" She began to sob through her words. "She took a few steps and fell to the ground. I could see her struggling to get up, but I couldn't seem to move to help her."

Dan listened as the words took shape in his mind. He could visualize the horror and empathized with the woman's sense of helplessness. "Like your feet were stuck in wet concrete?"

"Yes, it was just like that. I tried to move my feet to run, but they seemed so heavy."

"And she was still screaming, 'Somebody help my baby...'" Dan mumbled.

"That's exactly right! Dan, were you there?"

"I think... I... I remember that I had just eaten a rather large lunch, and I had a beer with it. I remember now... I was on my way back to the office." He glanced around the room. "A couple of co-workers, Kelley and... Chantal were with me. Oh no, they're over there!" He pointed across the room.

"Can you remember anything else?" She pressed him for more.

"I don't think they had finished eating. We were going outside to look for something... yes, that's it! Kelley had been watching the television over my shoulder. The sound was off so she was reading the closed captions. There was something about an unidentified aircraft that had been sighted directly over the downtown area."

"It must have been you standing next to me looking up at the sky. I don't think you had actually seen the accident." Ruth's eyes gazed into his, although he was staring just over her head as he tried to recall the event.

"I remember there was a beam of light shining down from the sky on the sidewalk. Oh my god! It... it... it was like it was dissolving everyone in its path as it came. Then it hit us... and I woke up here." He looked directly at the old woman. "I think we are inside the ship, or whatever it was that was up there."

They grew silent as they looked around at the people lying on the floor all around them. In a language neither of them understood, a voice suddenly sounded. They jumped at the ear-piercing noise, and Dan covered his ears as he tried to see where it was coming from.

When the strange message ended, he could still hear it swirling and repeating in his head. Each time, it was repeated in a different language. At first, it sounded like Chinese, and then French, followed by Italian or maybe Spanish, he wasn't sure. He recognized something like the Russian actors he had heard in a movie recently, but it did not matter what language it was, he still couldn't understand.

He looked down at the floor as the room started to shake and people began to sink into the middle, sliding slowly downward until they were gone. From where he stood, it appeared they were sinking as they might, if in quicksand. He could make no sense of it until he saw the funnel-like hole in the floor, which had opened up beneath them.

A terrible grinding sound rose from the void

below. That was bad enough, but he was horrified when a severed leg bounced up from the blackness. It flipped in the air before falling into the hole again.

With the strange message still reverberating in his head, he reached for Ruth. "Grab my hand. Close your eyes and hold on tight."

He sprang up and pulled the woman to her feet. Wrapping his arm around her waist, he lifted her feet off the floor. Clumsily, he carried her, stepping over and on the bodies around them as he scrambled for the wall. Behind him, he heard a woman screaming. It was a rattling sound, as though she was being shaken, cut short as the grinding blades swallowed her up.

When Dan reached the wall, he turned back toward the center of the room, setting her feet on the floor beside him. He pressed his back against the wall to try and avoid slipping, using one arm to help brace the old woman. The hole in the floor continued to expand toward the walls. It was mere moments before Ruth slipped away, struggling to reach out to him as she slid away into the void, her screams a faint echo as she disappeared.

At last, the swirling voice in his head began its message in English,

"We thank you for your sacrifice that we may

continue on our journey. You have been selected as an offering to insure the survival of your people. You are a brave and honorable contributor to your species."

As the final word echoed in his mind, the floor below him fell away. His screams were cut short as he joined the others passing through the processor and into the vat of human hamburger below.

The Inspiration for Hamburger:

The day we went to Decatur, we stopped for lunch at the Raging Burrito. As I was eating, I was taking in the atmosphere of the place. The old brick walls gave me the sense of being in the basement of an old house. I imagined being locked in there with the other patrons, not knowing how I got there.

After we finished eating, we walked a few blocks to the Dancing Goats Coffee Bar and were disappointed that it was not the trendy place we had expected. The more standard franchise environment tweaked my story setting into a more sterile kind of room, and not of this earth.

The noisy coffee shop was crowded with people, and so became the room where my characters were trapped. Of course, in that scenario the aliens had simply arrived at lunch hour to pick up some food when they plucked the unsuspecting victims from the sidewalk. It was as though they had just stopped by an intergalactic drive through.

Open For Business

Written at Java Joe's
Clarkesville, GA.

On the roads less traveled, small town America often holds on to the past with the same strong willed grip as do the well-seasoned citizens who inhabit the old brick buildings that line each Main Street. Some towns make an effort to modernize in order to keep the young people from moving away, while others try to restore the charm of the town to attract tourists. Sadly, some ultimately crumble to dust from neglect.

For many years, the residents of Rolandville feared that the town, where they had lived their entire lives, would fade away in a whisper. The broken glass of the storefront windows, the weeds that pried their way into every crack, and other omens of bad fortune struck them with a dark sadness. One day, the city council held a meeting and voted to do everything possible to rebuild the historic area around their beloved Main Street. Soon there were small shops and trendy restaurants moving into the broken shells of the rundown buildings and working with the town to breathe new life into them.

Sarah and her husband, Ray, were determined to find the perfect spot to open a boutique coffee house, and Rolandville was the first town they had come across that was in the process of revival, but still affordable. The place possessed the old Victorian appeal they were seeking. It appeared to be a decent location in which to reboot their lives. So, it was an easy decision to buy the building that previously housed the town's old hardware store.

After six months of hard work, stripping and refinishing the classic wooden floors, clearing trash and painting, they were nearly ready to open. They ran ads in the local paper announcing the grand opening and even had a special ceremony when the carved wooden sign was hung above the door. After years of dreams and discussions, their vision of *Java, the Hut* had become a reality at last.

Outside, an old man stood below the sign scratching his head and reading out loud, "Java, the Hut... I don't get it."

"It's a play on words, Dad," Ray said over his

shoulder. "It's from Star Wars."

"What wars? I don't remember any war like that. I was in the Big One and the only *stars* I saw were in the night sky over Normandy."

Ray laughed, "No, Dad, Star Wars was a movie that came out some time ago."

"A movie, you say? I didn't see that one. Last movie I saw was the one about... well, it had John Wayne in it."

"John who?" Ray was bent over and dragging the half-barrel of flowers into its place near the door. "There. How does this look?"

"It looks fine, son. Do you mind if I wait for you in the truck? I'm feeling kinda tired."

"Sure I'm almost done here for today, I guess. Everything is just about ready for tomorrow's grand opening."

Grabbing the broom that was leaning against the brick exterior, he swept the dirt that had fallen from the flowerpot into the street. He waited to make sure his dad got to the truck safely before he went inside to check on Sarah.

"Hey, babe." He hugged his wife and kissed her ear. "You just about ready to head out?"

"Not really. I still have to unpack the new cups and wash up the plates. Oh, and all the machines need to be cleaned again before morning. I have to run some water through them at least."

"Oh. I thought you already did all that. Dad was complaining about being tired. He's waiting in the truck. I think he is ready to go home and lay down for a nap."

Sarah looked disappointed. "I really need to finish this tonight. I don't want to panic in the morning when people start coming in."

"Well, I could take him home and come back. I'm sure he wouldn't mind. I mean… we *are* opening our new business in the morning. He should expect us to have a few things to finish up."

She was trying to open one of the boxes that lined the floor behind the counter. He stepped up to help.

"There you go." He took a knife from his pocket, cut the last of the packing tape from the top and opened the flaps of the box. "Okay, I'm going to take him back to the house and be back in about a half hour. We can grab some take-out for dinner before we go home. Dad will probably be ready to eat by then."

"That sounds good. I just hope the restaurants are still open if we're late." She started pulling the coffee mugs from the box and lined them up on the counter.

"Wow, I didn't know those were going to be green." Ray picked up a mug and held it up to the light.

"Well, Jabba the Hut is green, right? What did you think I would get?"

Ray shrugged his shoulders and turned to leave. "I don't know, baby, maybe Storm Trooper white. Anyway, it doesn't matter. I'll be back soon. Don't worry, I'll lock the door on my way out."

"Bye, honey. Drive careful," she called out to him as he pulled the door shut behind him. She smiled when the bells on it chimed and a solid click meant he'd turned the key in the lock.

As Ray climbed into the truck, he found his father leaning his head against the window and snoring. Rather than wake him, he started the truck and began driving back to the house. He let his mind wander back to the days when they had first come to Rolandville.

The realtor that helped them find their building was a pleasant, older woman. She'd lived in the town most of her life, so she enjoyed telling the younger couple stories about its history.

***

"That's the place where they used to celebrate the autumn festival." She pointed at a rock in a grassy yard in front of a building.

"They don't do that anymore?" Sarah leaned forward from the back seat.

"There's been talk about bringing it back, maybe this year." About a hundred yards later, she pointed through the windshield. "That is where they hung the Thompson brothers for murder."

She stopped at the 'Y' intersection for a long moment and looked up at the branches of the tree. "They say they kicked and jerked for near ten minutes afore they finally died. Some very bad boys, the old folks say."

Ray had been keen to hear more, but Sarah seemed upset by the story. She tried to turn the focus back to their original mission, asking a few questions about the listing of the old hardware store. "I see that the store has been vacant for many years. Why is that?"

"Well, it was originally built in 1852. Back then it was the post office, the only one for more than two hundred miles. Of course, in those days the town was surrounded mostly by forest. However, Rolandville was the county seat, so a lot of the government buildings were here."

She drove these streets effortlessly, looking out the car windows and at Sarah in the rearview mirror as though she need not watch the road. "That's why the hanging was back at the place I pointed out to you. Used to be a courthouse right there before it burnt down. The sheriff and the judge made quick work of the whole business. You see, the Thompson boys killed that sheriff's wife when they robbed the post office. After that, it was moved into a new place and the building sat empty until the hardware store opened during the war, around 1940 I guess it was. Old man Taylor ran it for more than sixty years until he died in 2004."

She braked suddenly and blew the horn at a dog standing in the road. "Not much was happening here then, so they just boarded it up and it's still empty today. It's going for next to nothing. Want to take a look?"

Taking the realtor's recommendation, they stopped to see it. At the first sight of the building's interior layout and exposed brick walls, Sarah fell in love with the space.

***

Just as Ray pulled into the driveway of the old house, his father awoke.

"Where are we?" he asked, rubbing his eyes and looking around.

"We're home, Dad."

"Where's… uh… the girl?"

"You mean Sarah? She's finishing up. I need to go back and help her."

"Well, before you go, you think we could get something to eat?"

"I'm gonna bring food back after I get Sarah. Can you wait?"

"Sure, son. Just leave me a couple packs of sugar in case I have a seizure. I had my insulin about an hour ago. Don't worry, I'll be okay… here… alone." The old man's voice trailed off.

Ray felt pangs of guilt. He was hungry too. He had ignored the feeling for hours, but his father's almost pathetic request had reminded him. He helped the old man out of the truck.

"What do you say we raid the fridge?"

They headed into the house to see what they could find.

***

Sarah was in the back room tying up a trash bag when she heard the bells on the door chiming. She dropped the bag and walked through the doorway to the shop. "I'm glad you're back, honey. We can get this done quicker if…"

She stopped, realizing there was no one else

in the shop. Looking around, she walked to the door. She thought Ray had locked it when he'd left. Sure enough, when she pulled at the handle, the door was still solidly locked.

That's weird. It must have been a draft. She blew a puff of air at the bells but they did not move or make a sound. Whirling around at the sound of a crash from behind her, she gasped at the sight of two of her new coffee cups smashed on the floor.

"What the heck?" She walked over to get a closer look at the rest of the cups left sitting on the counter. *Is the counter not level?* She placed both hands on the smooth surface and bent over to look at it from the side. There was no good reason why the cups would have slid off. "I don't get it."

She walked around the counter to get the broom and dustpan to sweep up the pieces. Using the pan, she pushed the broken ceramic mugs into a pile. Just as she began to sweep the mess into it, the remainder of the mugs flew off the counter, some of them hitting her before crashing to the floor. Shrieking and backing away, she dropped the broom and tried to cover her head.

"Whoever you are, my husband is on the way."

She backed further from the mess and looked around for her phone. It was not on the counter where she thought she had left it. Staying as far from the counter as possible, she made for the back room and looking around, spotted it on one of the metal racks there. She snatched it up and pressed the button to wake it, but it remained dark. She smacked it against the palm of her hand and tried the button again, but nothing happened.

From inside the main room of the shop, a loud rustling made her heart skip a beat. Gathering her courage, she walked to the doorway and leaned out with her back against the doorframe. All of the new tables and chairs had been moved to the center of the room and were stacked to the ceiling. It was an impossible structure. The legs of chairs were sticking out in every direction. Then as she was watched, the precarious stack collapsed into a mangled pile on the floor.

Shaken, Sarah dropped the phone. She thought of escaping through the back door, but she remembered it was locked and she did not have a key for it. The locksmith wasn't scheduled to come until the next day to change the lock, so for now, the steel door was as good as a wall. With no windows in the storeroom, there was no other way out but through the front door.

She stood frozen. She needed to get moving before anything else happened. Looking through the doorway again, she strained to see if there was a clear path to the front door. With a sudden screeching and banging, the metal shelves behind her began to empty themselves. Shelf by shelf, the contents flew across the room until all them were emptied and knocked over. Her heart was pounding in her head as she backed slowly through the door and out toward the main room.

From her right, a blast of steam seared her arm and she screamed in agony. She did not remember turning the espresso machine on, but it was cranking out a cloud of steam as it floated through the air toward her. It was nearly upon her when the electric cord caught on the water faucet and stopped its progress.

Now, she was really panicked and backed away stumbling until she was stalled by the wall directly behind her. Waves of fear washed over her and she was finding it difficult to move. In the cloud of steam, she could plainly see the forms of two very large men taking shape. Staring up at them, she began to make out their faces as their bodies faded into view. She gasped when she saw the telltale red lines around their necks. Rope burns!

"The Thompson Brothers?" The words

escaped in a gasp before the breath could return to her lungs.

She broke for the door, but found it locked. She shook the handle as though somehow she could shake it loose. Then out of the dark, something grabbed her from behind, and she could sense strong hands lifting her from the floor. She let out a blood-curdling scream as she was forcefully pulled back and then thrown through the glass of the door and onto the sidewalk outside.

For a moment, she lay crying on the cold concrete. She brought her hand up to feel her head and pulled it back to see her blood covered fingers. Struggling to stand, she looked around for someone who could help her, but there was no one in sight. The entire street was abandoned.

Looking through the broken glass of the door, she yelled back inside, "You blew it! I'm still alive." Laughing wildly, she added, "You tried to stop me but you failed. You idiots can't even…"

The heavy wooden sign above the door swayed loosely back and forth. With a cracking noise, the bolts holding it in place broke free and it fell directly on the bloodied woman standing below, crushing her to the sidewalk.

Only a few moments later, Ray returned to the coffee shop. Finding Sarah crushed on the sidewalk, the broken pieces of the sign surrounding her, he desperately tried to save her. As he bent over her shattered body, he noticed something beneath her hand. It was written in blood, her index finger pointing at it as though she were punctuating the message. He moved her hand gently to reveal...

"SORRY. WE'RE CLOSED."

The Inspiration for Open For Business:

We met Susan's parents that day in Clarksville and had lunch at The Copper Pot before heading over to Java Joe's. I had seen photos of the place on the web and was surprised at how small it was inside. The sign that hung outside and the name of the place gave me the inspiration for the shop in the story, but it was the age of the town itself, and the obvious efforts to revitalize it, that gave me the heart of the story.

I could imagine the days when punishment came swift and judgment was limited to a handful of people. Shortly after we finished our coffee, Susan went on a walking tour with her parents and I stayed behind to create the story you just read.

For Another Day

Written at Hodgepodge Coffee
Atlanta, GA

Jude sat on the sofa sipping his latte and looking about the room. Under the table, his foot was shaking nervously as the tone on his phone indicated yet another incoming message. He squirmed on the soft cushions knowing he had better think of a good excuse to offer the man he was supposed to be meeting here. It had only been two days since they had first met, but it seemed like an eternity.

On Wednesday, he had been sitting in this very same spot, contemplating putting an end to his miserable life. He was trying to find anything to justify his continued existence and it was nearly impossible to think of any reason to go on living. After his recent string of bad luck, he had been suffering from a profound sense of hopelessness.

The trouble had begun several weeks earlier when he had lost his job. His girlfriend, Tanya, had promised to pick up the slack and cover the rent and the rest of the bills until he found something. It seemed like a good arrangement, but then she left him after he got stoned and inadvertently left their apartment door open. Her cat had run out into the street only to be crushed by a beer truck. For her, it was the last straw. To make matters worse, he was evicted from the place just two weeks later and had been sleeping in his car ever since.

None of that mattered now. He was here to meet this man, whose name he could not remember, and these were to be his last moments on this earth. He reflected on all of the other times he had contemplated suicide in the past. There were several occasions when all had seemed hopeless to him. There was the period following his mother's death, and again when his first wife had left him only three months after their wedding.

"I can't deal with all your whining," she yelled before slamming the door and disappearing into the night.

He had felt like shit then, but now it was worse. Things had piled up, and two days ago, he hit the bottom of his worthless life.

***

"Hello, my friend. I sense there have been better days. May I sit?" The stranger nodded toward the empty space on the sofa. "My name is Finnity. You can call me Finn."

Jude stared down at his feet, which were resting on the heavily painted coffee table. He wasn't sure what the man had said but guessed it was something about sitting there. "Yeah, sure."

"Listen, friend, I have a pressing appointment in the next hour, but I was wondering if you know of anyone who could use a few thousand dollars, perhaps ten thousand or so."

That got Jude's attention. He sat up to study the man's face. "Did you say ten thousand dollars? Are you for real? For what?"

"I know it's odd for a stranger to walk in and talk money, but I'm a man of few words when it comes to doing business. I go straight for the kill, you could say." Finnity followed the statement with a stilted laugh.

"What kind of business are you in? Are you looking for a hit man or something?" Jude moved as far away from the man as he could without actually standing to walk away. His pulse quickened and it made him feel somewhat dizzy.

"Oh no, nothing as dramatic as that." The stranger laughed. "As a matter of fact, I am in the life extension business. I help people, especially those who are suffering."

"Like with cancer or something?"

"Many of my clients have been stricken with cancer, yes." The man scratched the stubble on his chin. "Others have been victims of terrible accidents. The reasons are many and I really don't have the time to…"

"Funny, your clients want to extend their lives, and right now I could give a damn about mine." Jude stared out the window to avoid looking at the man's face.

"I see. I guess that is why I was drawn here this afternoon, Jude. I was passing by and I sensed your need. You were searching for an answer and didn't even know I could help you. Isn't fate amazing?"

"How do you know my name?" Jude wasn't sure if he had actually heard the man say his name or only imagined it.

"Why, you must have told me. It doesn't really matter." Finnity extended his hand across the table to grasp Jude's with a firm grip. "All that matters is that I can help you with the pain you are experiencing. At least for a short while, you could be a very rich man."

"What, ten thousand dollars?" He jerked his hand away from the man's cold grasp. "What would I have to do?"

"Why, you don't have to do anything at all. If you agree to the terms and conditions, I will give you the money right now. In forty-eight hours, you will meet me back here and I'll collect the time you have left here in this world. You will have the solution to your problem, and my client will have... wait a moment..."

He pulled a device from his pocket and appeared to punch a few keys on it, "My client will have an additional forty-six years, ten hours, five minutes and thirty-two seconds added to her life. Right now, she only has three days, forty-five minutes left." He returned the device back to his pocket and smiled

"Who the hell are you, the damn grim reaper?"

"Oh no, Jude. Do I look grim? I am a businessman. If you do not wish to have your burden lifted, I apologize, and I'll be on my way." The stranger turned to leave.

Jude reached out to take hold of the man's arm. "Finn, wait. Please."

"Yes?"

"So you'll give me ten thousand dollars right

now, and in forty-eight hours I give you the rest of my life? Is that right?"

"Yes, that is correct."

"I only have one question… will it hurt?

"No, not at all. You will feel increasingly drowsy until you are simply… gone. I assure you, it is entirely painless. In fact, most of my donors are smiling in their final moments."

"I'll… I'll do it then."

"Think carefully, my friend, there are no second chances. When your time ends, I will be there, wherever you are. There is no hiding, no changing your mind. My agreement is one hundred percent binding and non-cancellable."

"Look, man, I don't have anything left to lose. No one even cares if I'm around anymore. What's next? What do I have to do?"

Finnity hesitated and looked deep into Jude's eyes. "I can see you are ready to make the deal."

Once more, he pulled his device from his pocket, flipping open a panel near its base. "Just place the index finger of your right hand on the pad and hold it there for a moment." He extended the device to Jude and waited.

Jude pulled at the older man's wrist to look more closely at the strange gadget. There were no buttons on it. It appeared to be constructed from a solid piece of black plastic or glass, except for the open panel with a small cover that was pulled back. He hesitated, looked up at the man and placed his finger on the pad.

"Ouch! Did something bite me?" He let go of the man's arm.

"That was your signature." The man placed the device back in his jacket pocket. From the same pocket, he pulled ten stacks, each of ten one hundred dollar bills.

Was it possible for all of that to be stuffed into one pocket? Jude began to have anxiety again.

"Here you are, my friend. The time stamp is 2:36 PM. I will see you in exactly two days. Same place, and of course, at the same time. Agreed?"

As he placed the stacks on the table, Jude was already gathering them up. He stuffed the bills into the pockets of his jeans and jacket, promising, "I'll be here."

When he looked back up, the man was gone. He felt strange, as though he had just imagined the whole scenario. He reached down and touched his pocket. Yes, the money was still there. Best of all, it was real.

***

That was forty-seven hours and fifty minutes ago. In the time that had elapsed, Jude experienced something quite unexpected. The money had changed the way he saw his life.

The first thing he'd done was to call Tanya and apologize. He asked if he could see her one last time and she agreed. During that visit, she told him how sorry she was that she left him so abruptly. She had been missing him terribly ever since. She told him that she loved him and hoped they could get back together. After a long conversation and a lot of questions, he agreed to move into her new apartment and be with her again. He was so happy. He gave her half of his money and told her to hold onto it. It would be enough to cover their rent for next few months, at least until he could find work.

He wanted to use the rest to pay some debts to a few of his old friends, even though most of them had cut ties with him long ago. They had grown tired of his continual need for help. He borrowed money from them without ever offering to pay it back. He was sorry that his hard times had gotten in the way of their friendship, so he made some calls and asked them to meet with him later in the day.

Most of the friends were surprised to see him, and even more surprised to receive repayment of the money they had lent. Each told him how hard it had been to give him the boot. All were glad to hear that he had gotten his life on track again and wanted to stay in touch.

So it went for much of the two days he had been given. He even contacted his estranged father. They had not spoken to one another for years. As he ended the call, he promised his dad that they would get together soon.

Now his phone was going crazy with text messages and social media notifications from friends. He had not enjoyed such friendship for many years and he liked the way it felt. If only he was not haunted by the deal he had made, life would have been so good again.

Nevertheless, the stranger had said, "There are no second chances *When your time ends, I will be there, wherever you are... no hiding, no changing your mind...*" The agreement was binding and non-cancellable. He could remember it so clearly now, but no matter how hard he tried he could not remember the man's name.

A chirp from his phone, and another message from Tanya, simply, "Love you." He checked the time again. It was exactly 2:36. It was the agreed upon time and the man wasn't there. A wave of relief washed over him. The guy wasn't going to show! Looking around to be sure, he saw no one else in the coffee house but the employees. He felt the weight of the commitment fall away and smiled as he realized that he was free. Jumping up from his seat on the sofa, he turned to leave when a voice called to him from behind.

"Hello, Jude."

He spun on his heel and there stood the stranger, holding the device in his hand. "Life is good, yes?"

"I… how did you know? I wanted to talk to you about that. I was thinking, I still have some of the money and I could pay you back the rest if…"

"Ah! I see, my friend. You would like to cancel our agreement, even pay me back?"

"Yes, exactly. I could have it for you in a few months, I'm certain of it. I could make payments in the meantime if…"

The man held his finger up to stop him. "I know. I hear this every day, my friend. You have decided that you were wrong, that life is precious, and you want another chance to live it as was intended from the day you were born."

"Yes, but please understand that this is different. I didn't have anything to live for before, and now I do."

"The truth is, Jude, you have always had much to live for. You just couldn't see beyond your own misery that the possibilities were just waiting there for you... to go after them. Most of my donors come to the same conclusion in the end."

The man smiled, continuing, "My clients on the other hand... they know how precious life is. Their time is nearly over, and they are kicking and scratching with every breath to hold on. They want the future they know is waiting for them if only they had more time, and they are willing to give anything to live to see it."

"Look, man you can't do this. You can't kill me right here. I'll scream..." He clutched at his throat and continued to move his mouth without a sound. The barista glanced over to see him grasping at his own throat, but made no move to help him.

The man looked at his device. "I am sorry, my friend. I really must be going. To tell you the truth, I do feel your pain. I have been alone for ages, but I am duty bound to continue my work. Perhaps one day I too will be free from the bondage of this world, but for now, I must be going. My client is waiting."

Jude tried to scream as the man touched the device to his forehead. He felt nothing as his spirit was whisked away into the cold blackness of the object. As the last wisp of life drained, his body dropped to the ground.

"Somebody dial 911!" The barista yelled to another employee as he ran to the man who had just collapsed in the sitting area of the shop. "Tell them to hurry!"

He touched two fingers to the unconscious man's neck, but there was no pulse. He grabbed his arms and pulled to straighten him on the floor, and began administering CPR. After a few minutes, the rescuer gave up and sat down next to Jude's lifeless body.

Finnity stood back and watched the show as he had done many times before. He glanced at his watch. His cancer-stricken client was waiting for her extension on life, and he didn't want to be late. He stepped away, sighed loudly, and faded into the wall.

The Inspiration For Another Day:

Hodgepodge Coffee House and Gallery is a cool place housed in graffiti covered building just outside of metro Atlanta. When I first arrived, I ordered a fantastic brunch of scrambled eggs and cheesy grits, even though Susan had suggested I try the cinnamon roll waffle.

While eating in the main room, I took in the art hanging on the walls and from the ceiling, lots of skulls and gothic imagery. In an adjoining room, I could see a guy sitting by himself on the sofa. He kept looking anxiously at his watch. Though he was part of the inspiration for the story, it was the contrast in life views experienced by two people close to my family that made it all come together.

Come and See

Written at Walker's Pub and Coffee
Athens, GA

Stan sipped his coffee while he awaited the arrival of his friends. They were to meet at the coffee house early in the evening and then hit the bars on the strip until the last one closed down. Tonight was supposed to be guys only, and he didn't have a problem with that since it had been several months since he and Laura had broken up. Since then, he had not heard anything from her or any of their mutual friends.

Thinking back on the day she had told him it was over, he realized he should have seen it coming. She had been distant for weeks before she had made it official. She cancelled dates and came up with wild excuses each time. For instance, "My spirit isn't in the right place tonight, Stan," or, "The vibe I'm getting from you tonight isn't conducive for our emotional alignment."

"What does that even mean?" he asked out loud with a shrug. He looked around to see if anyone had heard him. Perhaps he should keep his thoughts to himself.

He had not argued with her about splitting up. Instead, he had given her some space, thinking that she would come around. She didn't. In fact, she had disappeared so completely she might as well have moved out of town or dropped completely off the planet.

"It would be nice if…" He was thinking aloud again when his phone rang. He looked at the number on the caller ID, but it wasn't familiar so he ignored the call until it had rung out. "Yeah, go to voice mail."

Seconds later, the sound of cascading bells signaled that there was a new message. He pressed the button to hear it.

Static on a phone message was rare, but this call was heavy with it and he was about to hang up when he heard the voice. It was Laura. She sounded hysterical.

"Stan… I need you, baby." Each part of the sentence crackled with interference. "I don't know where I am. They're coming back… please, help me!" The message ended abruptly.

He didn't know whether to be excited or pissed. Here she was, in trouble, so now she calls. He was listening to the message again when Jack strolled in and slid into the booth across from him. "Hey bro, what's…"

Stan held up his index finger to indicate that Jack should wait a minute. When he pressed the button to hang up, Jack smiled a wide grin.

"What's new, Stanley?" He knew his friend hated to be called by his full name.

Stan cast Jack a look of disdain as he hit the number to call back. As he waited for the connection, he answered, "Don't be a dick. I just had an emergency call from Laura and…"

He was cut short by a series of tones and a recorded voice saying, "The number you have reached is not in service. Please check the number and try again."

"What the…?" Stan hung up and pressed the number again.

"What's up, man?" Jack's smile had faded. "What's she want, to crush your skull this time? She sure did a job on your heart the last time you talked to her."

Stan shook his head. "That's weird. I called her right back on the same number she used to call me and both times the recording said the number was not in service."

"Maybe the phone is jacked up." He grinned again at his own pun. "Try dialing it straight this time."

"Maybe you're right." Stan looked at the number, trying to memorize it, moving his lips silently as he repeated it to himself before dialing.

Again, the recording came on telling him the number was not in service.

"Damn, I can't help you, Laura, if you don't tell me where you are, especially if I can't call you back!" He slammed his fist on the table then shook the hurting hand. "Damn that hurts."

"Chill, man. She isn't worth popping a knuckle over, let alone breaking your hand. If it's that important, she'll call you back." Standing, he patted Stan's shoulder. "Gonna get me a cuppa joe. Right back." He wandered over to the coffee bar.

Stan was staring out the window, remembering the places he and Laura used to go, imagining where she could be right now, when the phone rang again. This time he answered on the second ring. "Laura?"

Again, there was static.

"Laura, tell me where you are so I can come and help." There was only static in response.

He took the phone from his ear and looked at the number. It was the same number he had been trying. He heard a voice and slapped it back to his ear. "Laura?"

"We have her." The man's voice grated on his nerves like fingernails on a chalkboard.

"What do you mean? Where is she? What have you done to her?"

"Done? Why, we haven't done anything... she is simply here with us and she seems to think you can help her." Static roared from the earpiece drowning out what the man said next.

"What was that last part?" He almost yelled into the phone as if more volume would help him cut through the noise, and it did. The static stopped.

"Yelling at me will not make the situation better for Laura or for you," the man said coolly.

"Listen, you bastard, you tell me where you're holding her or I'll..."

"You will what, my friend?"

Stan got hold of himself. He had no idea where they were keeping his ex- girlfriend, only that she needed him. Whether he wanted to admit it or not, he wanted her back in his life. He looked up to see that Jack was back and sitting across from him, listening intently.

"Look, buddy," Stan spoke into the phone. "Just tell me what you want and I'll bring it to…"

"Want? I don't want anything except for her to stop talking about you. Maybe if you come, she will shut up about you. That's what I want."

Jack was mouthing, *what do they want?*

Stan waved his hand to silence his friend. "So tell me where you are."

The call disconnected with a click.

"What?" He sat back, stunned.

"What do they want?" Jack was intrigued.

"I don't know. The guy said all he wanted is for me to go to wherever they are, but he cut out and didn't tell me where it is."

"I don't like the sound of it. Like what if she got into drugs after she broke up with you. She might be hanging with some shady types these days. You said she got pretty weird toward the end…"

"I don't think it has anything to do with drugs. Look, if the guy calls me back. I'm going to go to wherever they're keeping her. I'd like you to be there to watch my back, but I understand if you'd rather not." He watched his friend's face for a sign of his intention.

"Nah, man, it's cool. I'll run with you. That's what friends are for, right? Backing you up and all that."

"Yeah, I'd do it for you," he answered, "Unless it was that red-headed chick. She was such a…"

His phone rang, and he answered it before the second ring. "Hello?"

"Hey, Stan, I don't think I'm gonna make it tonight. Carly isn't feeling well, and I promised I'd hang out with her at home. I hope that doesn't make me sound whipped or…" It was Mark.

"Sure man, no prob. Later." He didn't want to chance missing a call from Laura, so he hung up before saying good-bye and sat the phone on the table in front of him.

He looked over at Jack. "That was Mark. He can't make it. Carly is sick and …" His phone started ringing and vibrating on the table. Grabbing it, he pushed the button to answer, putting it to his ear.

"Hello?" He heard very little static.

The man on the other end answered, "Come to the old church on the edge of town. We will all be waiting."

"All? All who?"

The phone disconnected.

"Let's go." He finished his cold coffee and stood to leave.

"Where are we headed?" Jack asked.

"Old church, outside of town."

"That run down old place? What are they doing there?"

"I don't know, man. You coming or what?" Stan was in a hurry to get going.

"Yeah, get the car started, and I'm at your heels." Jack chugged the rest of his coffee, choking out the word, *"Hot!"* He followed his friend to the street.

***

The car's headlights cut through the thick fog as they turned up the drive to the old church.

"We used to talk about this place a lot when we were kids." Jack spoke in a hushed near-whisper as Stan pulled up close to the church and cut off the lights.

"Yeah, I remember. It used to freak us out wondering about all the creepy things that could be hanging out around here. Now I think we are about to find out if they really are."

A shiver ran down Jack's back at the thought of it. "Maybe we should wait until daylight."

"No, we need to do this now. Come on." Stan got out of the car and walked around to open the back. His softball gear was still in the trunk, and he grabbed two aluminum bats from the tangled mess of plastic bags and jumper cables.

Offering the taped end of one of the bats to his friend, Stan apologized, "I only have one flashlight." He reached back into the trunk, rifling around in some papers until he produced a large flashlight. He clicked the button on the handle, but the light failed to turn on.

"Let me try." Jack took the light from his friend and slapped the side of it with his hand several times until it lit. The beam struck Stan in the face. "Typical. Ever notice how they never work in movies either?"

Stan instinctively held up his arm to shade his eyes. "You hang on to it since you seem to know so much about flashlights. I'll lead. Just shine it out in front of us so I don't trip over something."

"Right, you go ahead. I'll be right behind you."

Stan walked carefully toward the church,

stepping over the tall grass growing in the spaces between the stepping-stones on the path. When they reached the steps, he asked Jack to shine the light behind them. Satisfied that they were not being followed, he stepped up to the door and tried it.

With a loud creaking sound, it began to open. Stan was trying to look inside through the gap, but just as there was enough space to step through the doorway, they heard a muffled scream behind them.

"That sounded like Laura! It came from over there in the cemetery." Getting a better grip on the bat in his hands, he ran toward the sound.

"Wait up, man." Jack followed. He strained to aim the beam from the flashlight ahead of his friend and it was bouncing along the ground. By the time he caught up to him, Stan had stopped and was looking around.

"I don't see anything but weeds, dead trees and headstones."

"Maybe we just thought we heard a scream. It could have been a raccoon or some other..." Jack stopped midsentence. "Is that a..."

Stan looked to see what his friend was looking at in the beam of light pointed toward the ground. "Phone." He bent over and pulled the cell phone from the dirt where it lay half-buried.

"How old do you think it is?" Jack asked as Stan tried the power button. "That isn't Laura's phone, is it?"

"No, she had a newer one last time I saw her. This one is older and it doesn't look…" He was cut off by another scream. This time, it was very close by, yet the sound was muffled. "Quick, give me the light."

As soon as the light was in his hands, he searched the area until he found the large hole in the ground. "Do you see it?"

"What is it… some kind of animal hole?"

"I think it's big enough to crawl into. What kind of animal makes a hole that big?" Stan stepped closer and could see that a light spilled out from the hole. The reddish glow was brighter than the beam from his light, but then it was gone. "She must be in there. Maybe it leads to some kind of tunnel under the church. What do you think?

"I don't know, man. What if it's a badger hole? Those things are crazy. They'll tear you up if they think you're threatening them. We should call the cops."

"We don't have time to wait for the cops, Jack. I'm going in. You can make the call if you want, but Laura needs my help. I'm afraid every second counts." He dropped to his knees. "Tell you what, if I'm not back in ten minutes, don't come after me. Just call the cops."

"You're my best friend, man. Of course, I'll come after you if you don't get back here damn quick. If all hell breaks loose, the cops won't get here in time to save your stupid ass."

"You're a good friend, Jack."

"You come out safe, bro."

Stan nodded and began crawling head first into the hole, which was just wide enough to fit his shoulders. He was halfway in when he stopped moving.

In the darkness, Jack could hear the hoot of owls calling to each other. The hum of traffic coming from over by the highway did not cover the dampened sound of someone talking. It leaked out around Stan's body at the edge of the opening.

Jack could see his friend squirming slightly before being yanked violently further into the hole. Another jerk and Stan's feet disappeared into darkness.

"Stan! What the hell?"

He bent over to look into the hole. Blood shot out at him like a fire hose, spraying him in the face, blinding him. He choked on the gusher and fell backwards, his head striking a low-lying tombstone. Now he lay unconscious, covered with his friend's blood.

A moment later, two rotting arms reached from the opening. Bony fingers took hold of his feet and silently pulled him down into the dark depths beneath the headstones where Laura and her friends were waiting.

The Inspiration for Come and See:

On the way to Walker's Coffee Shop & Pub in Athens, GA, we passed by many stone buildings that gave me the inspiration for some type of gothic tale. When we finally arrived at our destination, every table and booth was populated by laptop gazing young people.

Remembering back on my youthful days, it seemed natural to make the story about an expired relationship and a group of guys who planned on hitting the bars… and, of course, a bad outcome for my characters.

Artifacts

Written at Cool Beans Coffee Roasters
Marietta, GA

The fall festival seemed to come early this year and tables covered by tent-like structures lined the sidewalks. The town square was teeming with folks from near and far. Mostly they browsed, often stopping to talk, and creating a bottleneck that made it difficult for others to pass.

"Gah! This was a mistake." Vasil stepped over a beagle that was lying with its head on its paws in the shade under a tree. He wished he had asked Katryn to meet him somewhere else this afternoon.

"Excuse me, sir," an elderly woman called out from her table. "You don't look to be from around here. I haven't been having much luck today, and you look like a man who has an appreciation for very fine and unusual things."

"What? Did you say something?"

"I said you look like a man who may be interested in the unusual, yet tasteful object of art." She smiled and revealed the years of yellowing enamel in her sparsely toothed smile.

"You're right, I do like art. I dabble in painting. My mother used to tell me she loved my work, but warned if I pursued it as a career, I would end up living under a bridge. So I do it now as more of a hobby."

"I knew it. I have a sense for the masterful creators of art. Sometimes it seems that I can feel it even a mile away. It can be overwhelming at this kind of event." She mopped sweat from her brow with a lace-trimmed handkerchief. "If I wasn't financially challenged at the moment, I would probably be relaxing at home right now with my cat in front of the fan."

Vasil looked over the items on her table. Now that he was focused more on what was in front of him than on the noisy crowd around them, he had to agree that she did have some of the most unusual objects he had seen at any festival table.

There were several religious icons, wooden crosses with various carved designs, small hand painted vignettes with hand modeled people posed in various activities, and other novelties. The one that caught his eye above the rest was a clawed foot from some type of bird. It was clutching a large crystal in its talons and the entire thing was mounted on a wooden carved base.

"Your eyes, they are so dark and mysterious, what is your heritage?" she inquired of him as he gazed at the crystal.

An unusual question from a stranger, he thought. Suddenly he had a distinct sense of déjà vu. It took a moment to overcome the strange sensation, but then he replied, "My family is from Bulgaria, but I was born here. I've lived most of my life in this town, except for a time when I attended the university in Savannah."

"For a time?" She turned and smiled at a woman who had stepped up to the table.

"Yes, my father fell ill, and I was called back home to be with him in his last weeks. He passed about six months ago."

"I am sorry for your loss. Losing a parent can be one of the most difficult losses. Were you close?"

"Yes, in the years before I went off to school, we spent a lot of time together. He was, perhaps, my best friend. We understood each other."

"A comfortable relationship then." Her eyes followed the female patron as she turned and walked away. Now she could give him her full attention again.

"That's a very nice way to describe it, comfortable. I like that. It was, indeed, a comfortable relationship." Vasil picked up the object and examined it from every angle as he spoke.

"I see you are interested in the crystal. My husband found it in a wooded area a few months before he passed. He claimed it fell from the heavens. He made the base from a small piece of rare wood he found nearby and spent many hours sanding it into the shape you see now."

"From what kind of bird was the claw taken?"

He looked closer at it as he now supposed it was an actual claw. Earlier, he had thought it might be molded from some plastic material.

"I don't pretend to know the answer to that. I had a book of birds and tried to find one that might match it, but came up with nothing. I'm not even sure it *is* a bird's claw."

Now Vasil was truly intrigued with the

object. If it was not from a bird, what kind of animal could it be? "How much are you asking for it?"

"I had considered how to charge for my goods, but ultimately, my heart has told me to allow my customers to price them. What value would you place on such a unique object?"

She waited for his reply without speaking as he considered the answer to the question.

"I... know it must be a rare find, but I can't afford much. How about... wait a minute." He pulled his wallet from his pocket, opened it, and counted the colorful bills inside. "Do you take plastic?"

"I am sorry that I cannot."

"In that case, I only have twenty-four dollars in cash. I'm sure it's not..."

Her face lit up as if he had just made her an excellent offer, and he wished he had offered her twenty.

"That would be fine. Would you like me to wrap it for you?"

"Ah... yes, please."

He watched as she pulled a sheet of waxy brown paper from beneath her table. It was wrinkled as though it had been used many times before. As she carefully wrapped the claw in the paper, she explained, " I am using this special paper because it will preserve the magical properties of the crystal. It must always be kept this way, especially at times of the solstice." Pulling a long piece of golden string from her pocket, she wrapped it one way, twisted it, and then crossed the first wrap to tie it off with a tight bow.

"What is it about the solstice that makes it so important?"

"That is when it is most powerful. You will see. I am so glad you came along. Only an artist such as yourself could appreciate such a find." She held out one hand for the money while she transferred the object to him.

At first, he was hesitant to take the wrapped claw from her, but then he thought about what she said about its power. What kind of power might it hold? He handed her the bills and took the packaged object.

"Thank you so much, young man. Learn to wield the crystal wisely, as I never really understood exactly how it works. I only know the stories that my husband has told."

Vasil tucked the small package into his messenger bag, tucking it next to his tablet computer. He turned to walk away. Suddenly a whoosh of air struck his face and the scene around him blurred out of view. "What the hell?"

***

As the town came back into focus, he looked around. It appeared to be much later in the day, and he was nearly alone in the square, except for the vendors loading their trucks. He pushed up his sleeve to look at his watch. Unless he was dreaming, several hours had passed since he had stopped to talk to the old woman who was now nowhere to be seen.

"Katryn! She is gonna be so pissed." He pulled his phone from his pocket. When he pressed the button to awaken it, the login screen was filled with messages of missed calls. The next to the last call had a message attached, so he clicked it to listen.

"Vasil, I don't know why you would tell me to meet you in the square and then not even bother to show up. I think maybe you need some time to think about whether our relationship is still important to you. Please don't call me tonight, I need some time to think about this… alone." There was nothing more.

He was tempted to press the call back button, but he knew her. If she said not to call, she meant it. In conjunction with the rest of the message, calling her now would appear to her that had not heard her message, or worse, that he was disrespecting her. He decided to just put the phone back in his pocket and find something to eat.

The Burgermeister Café was open, and he ordered carryout. While he waited, he pulled the wrapped object from his bag and turned it over in his hands. He couldn't remember that it had been so neatly tied up. The old woman had done it so quickly, and then she was gone as were most of the other people.

"Vasil," the man at the counter called out. In his hand was a greasy white bag.

Back at his apartment, the bag from the restaurant lay on the table where he had tossed it. He sat on the small sofa examining the crystal. It was a fascinating piece that looked as though it had been naturally created in a perfectly symmetrical shape. It did not look man-made in any way. There were lines, tiny red ones, like veins inside of it. The claw that held it was solid as stone, but it wasn't made of any stone he had seen before. It was rigid, but soft to the touch. He had removed the wooden base and it lay on the coffee table in front of him.

"Where do you come from?" he wondered aloud as he stared into the facets of the crystal. "What kind of power do you hold?"

Almost in answer to the question, a beam of light shot from the crystal and an image began to take shape on the wall. It was Katryn and she looked upset. She stood in the town square holding her phone to her ear. Shoving it into her purse, she turned to walk away just as a man approached. He smiled at her and took her by the hand. She returned his smile and kissed him on the cheek. After a few moments of conversation, which he was unable to hear, the two of them walked out of view and the image faded into the blank wall.

Vasil was stunned and angry. Who was this guy that was meeting with his girlfriend while he wasn't around? Was he the reason she needed some time to consider their relationship? There was not much opportunity to think about it, as suddenly he felt overwhelmed with exhaustion. He laid back on the sofa and instantly fell asleep.

A notification from his phone brought him back from the pit of darkness. He had no idea how long he had been sleeping, but at least he felt rested. He checked the coffee table for the crystal, but it wasn't there. Frantically, he searched the floor, but it was nowhere to be found. He thrust his hand down behind the cushion of the sofa and was relieved to feel the shape of the clawed crystal. When he pulled it out, he examined it all over again.

"What are you?" He turned it right side up. "Did you show me what was really happening?"

He did not expect a response, but just as before, a beam of light shot to the wall. At first blurry, the picture faded into view. Katryn was groaning and gyrating her hips to move against the man she was straddling. They were in her apartment on the kitchen floor and the rug beneath them was sliding back and forth, as she ground her pelvis against him.

Vasil threw the crystal across the room, yelling profanities as it bounced off the wall where the image had been projected. He felt a sharp pain in his head as the thing fell to the floor. Screaming in agony, he put his hands to his temples. Then he remembered how the old woman had warned him to keep the object wrapped in the paper. Taking the wrapper from the table, he crawled across the floor.

He carefully wrapped the paper around the claw and crystal, tying the string as he remembered the old lady had done. As he pulled the knot tight, the pain in his head was suddenly gone. Quickly, he went outside to the alley and threw the package and the wooden base in the dumpster before heading off to Katryn's apartment.

***

As he stood on the small stoop of Katryn's building, he tried to recover control of his emotions. When he felt he was calm enough, he pushed the plastic button to ring the doorbell. Swinging the door open, she looked surprised to see him.

"Vasil, I thought I would never see you again." She threw her arms around his neck and hugged him. "I am so sorry I left you those messages last month. I've been trying to call you to apologize, but you never answered your phone. When I came to your place, and you didn't come to the door, I was afraid you had left town."

"Last month? It was only yesterday." He was confused.

Katryn invited him in and again put her arms around him. As her hands slid down to his hips, she felt something bulging in his back pocket. Before he realized what she was up to, she had fished out the wrapped package and was stepping back to look at it. She turned the object in her hands. The string that held the wrapper in place loosened and fell to the floor.

A white glow from the crystal lit up her face, and she asked, "What is this?" She held it by the twisted stem of the clawed foot.

Vasil was stunned. "How did...?"

"What is it?" She continued to stare into the crystal.

"What day is it?" He asked, trying to grab the thing from her hands.

"It's the twenty-first. Why?"

"Never mind. Please give me that thing. I need to get rid of it."

She held it off to the side so he could not take it from her and coyly asked again, "What is it? I'm not giving it back until you tell me what it is."

"Honestly, I don't know. I bought it from an old woman the day I was supposed to meet you at the festival." He tried to maneuver closer to her to pluck it from her hand.

"Old woman? This is such a strange piece. What kind of a claw is this?" She pulled at it and the crystal began to glow a bright red.

"No! Don't mess with it! I don't know what it does, but it isn't safe."

Suddenly, the room seemed to tilt on its side. Katryn stretched before him like a long rubber band. Her terrified face was illuminated in the red light that emanated from the crystal. A second later, and with a BOOM like the sound of thunder, she was gone and so was the room.

***

"Gah! This was a mistake." Vasil stepped over a large poodle that was lying with its head on its paws in the shade of the fountain. He wished he had asked Katryn to meet him somewhere else this afternoon.

"Excuse me, sir," an elderly woman called out from her table. "You don't look to be from around here..."

The Inspiration for Artifacts:

On the day we went to Cool Beans Coffee Roasters, in Marietta Square, GA, there was a chalk art festival set up in the square. Since we usually eat and then go to the coffee house to work, I didn't take much time to look at the drawings, but I could see the booths and the many people strolling about to take in the sights.

While I was getting my work area set up at the table, a longhaired young man walked up to us and began a conversation. His name was Vasil, and he told us that he was an artist – a painter. He had noticed Susan taking photos and that I was setting up a place to work on my story. We spoke of art and the inspiration for it. He told me that he could sense other creative souls around him. Before he left, I asked if I could use his name for the story.

By the way, Vasil is from Bulgaria. Search for Vasil Vasilev Art to find his Facebook page and tell him I sent you.

Good to the Last Drop
Written at Café 45 South
Norcross, GA.

"Are those church bells I hear?" Cara asked as she wound her way down the narrow path. She stepped carefully to avoid making shadows in the moonlight that washed over the stone steps that led to the water. The lunar glow was all that kept her from tripping on the uneven ground.

"I think so, although I've never heard them before. I haven't been out here around midnight either." Mark would have rather blamed the chilled air for the goose bumps on his arms. The sound of the bells had come unexpectedly, and if he were to be honest, it freaked him out.

"This is so exciting, to think that there might be ghosts out here. Who did you say told you about this?" She waited for him to catch up to her and took him by the hand.

"I read it in a magazine called *American Haunts*. The article stated that there are several ghosts here, usually seen around midnight. Apparently, there are spirits of several teenagers who drowned in a boating accident near here in the 1950's. On the night of the prom, they'd come to the lake to party with some friends in their father's boat. Sometime after setting out from shore, their boat flipped over. None of the bodies was ever recovered."

He spoke casually as though it didn't bother him, but it did. Thoughts of ghosts made him uneasy. He wouldn't even be out here tonight if he didn't think Cara might be impressed.

The last ring of the bells sounded. Midnight had arrived. "That's it then. We should find a place to sit along the bank. We can wait there and watch to see if they appear."

He looked around in the dim glow of the moonlight and spotted a large rock close to the water. "Over there looks good."

"Yeah, that's what I was thinking." She pulled him along as if she was in a hurry to sit down. When they got to the large flat rock, she pulled a blanket out of the tote bag she was carrying and spread it over the surface of the cold stone.

"This is a nice spot, Mark. I couldn't have chosen any better." She sat down on the blanket and reached out. "Sit next to me."

There was no hesitation. He smiled as he settled down next to her. This was perfect. A bit creepy, perhaps, but perfect. It was exactly as he had hoped. No one was around to interfere. Maybe things would go his way tonight.

"Where was the boat supposed to have tipped over?" She scanned the water hoping to see some kind of a marker.

"Supposedly twenty yards or so out from the shore. Probably over there somewhere." He pointed toward where the moonlight was reflecting on the water. "This must be the spot because the pictures in the magazine showed this rock that we're sitting on."

"Even better then. I hope they come out tonight."

"According to the article, they have been seen many times by people who came out here to night fish after midnight. If there's any chance of them showing, it should be soon."

She moved closer to him and rested her head on his shoulder. He responded by putting his arm around her and holding her gently.

"This is so perfect," he mumbled.

"Oh, it is," she replied.

About a half hour later, there was a voice behind them.

"Hey, buddy, do you have a light?" The stranger held a cigarette in one hand and simulated using a lighter with the other.

"No, man. I don't smoke."

"You don't have to be a smoker to have a light. How about you, missy?"

"I think I might have some matches in my bag. Wait a sec."

Mark was frustrated by her willingness to help the stranger. Why did she have to encourage him?

"I didn't know you smoked." He watched as she pulled a box of wooden matches from her bag.

"I don't. It's like Paul said. You don't have to be a smoker to have matches." She handed the box to the stranger.

It took a moment for her words to sink in, but finally it registered. "Paul? You know this guy?"

"What? No, of course not."

"You called him Paul." He was staring at her, looking for a sign that she was lying.

"Did I? I don't know why. Is it a problem? It's probably not even his name."

Mark turned to the man and asked, "What's your name?"

"Does it matter?" He took a drag from the cigarette and tossed the box of matches on the blanket.

"It does if your name is Paul."

"Alex. My name is Alex."

"See. His name is Alex. Do you feel better now?" There was a sarcastic tone to her voice.

"I don't know." He considered for a moment whether he felt better about it or not. After all, it wasn't as if he knew her very well. He had only met her about a week ago; although he had been strongly attracted to her from the moment their eyes had met.

"So whatcha doing out here tonight, anyway. Away from all the lights and people?" The man took a long drag from the cigarette and blew the smoke out through tight lips.

"We're taking a break from…" Mark started but was cut off mid-sentence.

"Looking for ghosts," Cara volunteered. "They come out around here after midnight."

The stranger roared with laughter. "Did he

tell you that?" He coughed a couple of times. "Sounds like a line of crap to me. I think he brought you out here to try to get into your pants. That's what I think."

Mark was angry now. The guy was right, but it was not what he wanted to hear from a stranger spouting off in the middle of the night, especially not on this night.

"Look, bud, why don't you just take your smoke and move along?"

"What, and leave you here alone with Cara?" He took another puff from the cigarette and threw it into the water. "Maybe you're a crazed rapist or something."

Mark stood and faced the man. "How do you know her name?"

Turning to her, he demanded, "How does this guy know you?"

"I don't know. Maybe you mentioned my name, Mark." She batted her eyes at him in an exaggerated show of innocence.

"Not since he arrived I didn't." He looked suspiciously at her and then at the other guy. "What is this? Is he your brother or something? Did you bring a bodyguard along?"

The darkness was thick with silence.

"Cut the crap, Cara. Tell him why you

brought him here." The stranger pulled another cigarette from a pack and lit it with the one he had been smoking.

She turned quickly to stare at the guy, incredulous at what he had just said. "Why are you doing this? You've never done this before."

"Done what before?" Mark was pissed. He didn't like this new twist to the conversation. He looked at Cara and then turned to face the other man. "What the hell are you two up to?"

His anger was getting the best of him, and he did not see her reach into her bag. With one rapid motion, she pulled out a straight razor and lunged at him, swinging the razor at his heel.

"What the fu…" Mark screamed grabbing for his foot. She had sliced clean through his Achilles tendon.

As he began to lose his balance, she swung again and sliced the other tendon. Now he dropped to the ground screaming and thrashing. He grasped at his feet, struggling to stop the blood that was spurting from his heels.

"Come on, Paul. Just eat him and get it over with." Cara was crawling backwards away from Mark, trying not to get his blood on her clothes.

"Why are you doing this to me? You planned this, didn't you?" Mark moaned between clenched teeth.

The stranger leaned over him and smiled. "Oops, you caught us. Whatcha gonna do now, tough guy?"

Mark wanted to run, but his feet could not support him enough to stand. "Get away from me!" he yelled. "I'm gonna…"

"What? Scream? You already did that." Cara taunted him from a distance. "I don't think it matters at this point. Go ahead and scream."

"Aaaaaaaaaagggggggggggghhhhhhhhhhhhh!" Mark screamed, "Somebody help me!"

"Good try, but like she said, it's not going to help." Paul was leering at him. "You see, man, she's done this before. Many times, with many different guys and a few women too. Been that way since the first time she came here all alone a couple of years back. She was drunk when I came up on her. I was just about to eat her when she started to beg. Told me she'd do anything if I didn't kill her, and you know what? It seemed like a good idea, so I let her live."

He winked at her, as his features began to change. "I know where she lives, you know. I could just go and take care of her there if she didn't follow through with her promise. It doesn't matter at this point, I know where you lived too."

Mark was terrified as he watched the other man's body becoming increasingly grotesque. His mouth was elongating and distorting, the eyes on his face shrinking back into dark eye sockets. He spoke no more as his tongue lapped out over large spiked teeth.

"He told me to bring someone here once a month after midnight, and he would let me live. I do it. I have to do it, or he'll kill me instead. Like he said, he'd come to my house."

"Why the hell didn't you just move?" Mark whined as he tried to crawl away.

"Because I get to keep the money and stuff." She reached into his back pocket and snatched his wallet. "I don't date guys who don't have some money to spend."

She opened the wallet and scanned the contents. "Looks like I was right about you."

"You bitch!" he seethed. "You disgust me."

"No worries. Looks like Paul is ready for you now." She stepped back away from him. "Nice knowing you, Mark. I mean it. You seemed like a nice guy." She turned and walked away.

Mark let out a blood-curdling scream as the hideous creature jumped on him. The crunching sound of grinding bones echoed out across the lake in the darkness. In a few moments, the creature sat alone on the rock, its stomach bulging from the night's meal. Belching, it reached into its giant maw and pulled out a shoe, dripping with blood.

"Arrrggh," he growled. Holding the damaged shoe in his clawed hand, he held it up and drained the last drop of blood from it. When he was satisfied that it was empty he threw it twenty yards out into the deep dark water, scattering the reflection of the full moon on its surface.

The Inspiration for Good to the Last Drop:

We have been writing at Café 45 South for a couple of years, and a lot of good stories have come from it, as you can see. The inspiration for this story was in the title. Since it was the last story at the last coffee house on the tour, the phrase, "Good to the last drop," from the Maxwell House coffee commercials came to mind.

My stories often arise as an expansion of the title. For me, the title always comes first. Only rarely is it altered by the time of publishing, and then only slightly. As an example of this, my first novel was called, "The Box," until just before it was released. Unfortunately, about a month before I went to press, a SciFi thriller movie came out with the same name. Rather than appear to plagiarize, I simply added, "Spirit" to the title. Funny thing is, it turned out to be a better title, and I have never regretted the change.

Thank You

So, this is the end of the tour. I am glad you could come along. Don't fear, this is only the first tour. We had so much fun doing it, that there most certainly will be another in our future. I feel something in the air...

Don't forget to review this book on Amazon.com, GoodReads.com, and anywhere else a review can be posted, it does make a difference.